The Knight who was Afraid of the Dark

BARBARA · SHOOK · HAZEN

The KNIGHT WHO WAS AFRAID

OF THE DARK

PICTURES BY TONY · ROSS

A PUFFIN PIED PIPER

Published by Dial Books for Young Readers
A Division of Penguin Books USA Inc.
375 Hudson Street
New York, New York 10014

Text copyright © 1989 by Barbara Shook Hazen
Pictures copyright © 1989 by Tony Ross
All rights reserved
Library of Congress Catalog Card Number: 88-18149
Printed in U.S.A.
First Pied Piper Printing 1992
ISBN 0-14-054545-X
5 7 9 10 8 6 4
A Pied Piper Book is a registered trademark of
Dial Books for Young Readers,
a division of Penguin Books USA Inc.,
® TM 1,163,686 and ® TM 1,054,312.

THE KNIGHT WHO WAS AFRAID OF THE DARK
is also published in a hardcover edition by
Dial Books for Young Readers.

For the brightness Emily and Sarah bring

B. S. H.

Once long ago in a time known as the Dark Ages, there lived a bold and much loved knight. He was called Sir Fred.

He drove monsters out of the moat.

He chased the dishonest merchants out of town and saved the
fair Lady Wendylyn from a hideous ten-headed dragon.

There was only one crack in Sir Fred's armor. Sir Fred was afraid—knee-bumping, heart-thumping afraid—of the dark.

He was afraid of the dark of the moon, the dark at the top of the
steep stone stairs, the dark at the bottom of the big brass bed,
and the dark between the head hole and the arm hole when he
put on his armor.

Because he was afraid, Sir Fred kept his bedchamber bright with candles. He kept a bottle of fireflies on his knight table and slept with his pet electric eel,

whom he took with him if and when he had to get up to go to
the bathroom.

Sir Fred was also afraid of being found out. Indeed there was one who suspected. That one was the castle bully, Melvin the Miffed.

Melvin the Miffed couldn't stand Sir Fred because he was better loved, especially by Lady Wendylyn.

Melvin the Miffed stalked the castle corridors, sneaking and peeking and trying to find the crack in Sir Fred's armor.

Melvin the Miffed observed that Sir Fred did all his brave deeds in broad daylight. All the other knights liked the cover of darkness.

He also saw that Sir Fred was the only knight who did *not* cower under the Round Table during thunder and lightning storms. Indeed, the bolder the bolt, the better.

Moreover he observed that Sir Fred only met Lady Wendylyn
on nights when the moon was full, which was why they seldom
saw each other and why Lady Wendylyn began to wonder if she
was truly Sir Fred's True Love.

Things came to a head one dark day when Melvin the Miffed
sneaked up and peeked at a letter Lady Wendylyn was reading.
    "If your True Love truly wanted to see you," Melvin the Miffed
whispered, "he wouldn't make up silly excuses not to."

"Wicked good point," Lady Wendylyn said, tossing her curls and stamping her foot.

That afternoon Lady Wendylyn embroidered a banner and hung it out her window.

Sir Fred saw the banner and sank into deep despair.

The evening sky was exceedingly dark and the moon was thin as a mouse's whisker. Sir Fred pummeled his pillow and hemmed and hawed, "Oh, woe, shall I stay? Or shall I go?

"If I don't go, I will lose my ladylove because she will think I don't love her. If I do go, I will lose my ladylove because she will think I am scared of the dark, which I am."

In the end Sir Fred went. His fear was big. But so was his love.
He went armed with a fistful of fireflies, a glowworm-studded
shield, and his faithful electric eel wound around his arm.

Lady Wendylyn was waiting by the fountain with her eyes tightly closed. At the stroke of midnight she opened them and shrieked, "EEEEEEEEEEEEEEEEEEEEEEEK!"

As she shrieked, she grabbed Sir Fred's hands, released the fireflies, flung the shield to the ground, and tweaked the electric eel's tail light, leaving Sir Fred terrified in total darkness.

"EEEEEEEEEEEEEEK! Get off my True Love!" Lady Wendylyn shrieked again as she flicked a last lingering firefly from Sir Fred's sleeve.

"To tell the truth," she then said, "I'm terrified of bugs and all slithery things that creep and crawl."

Sir Fred then did his bravest deed. He told Lady Wendylyn the truth about himself. "I am," he admitted, "afraid of the dark— knee-bumping, heart-thumping afraid—of the dark."

"Then you are even braver than I thought," Lady Wendylyn said, flinging her arms around Sir Fred, "because you met me anyway."

"And you are brave as well as beautiful," Sir Fred said with a kiss, "because you tried to protect me."

Melvin the Miffed was still sneaking and peeking around. He saw the loving scene and snorted, "How sickening!" Then he stamped his feet and stalked off forever.

Nobody saw him leave. Lady Wendylyn was too busy patting
Sir Fred's electric eel and saying, "Hmmm, he's not as scary as
I thought."

Meanwhile Sir Fred was clutching his True Love and telling her,
"Hmmm, the dark's not so scary either. *With* someone."